Fairytales for Feminists

To guard against possible misrepresentation, if any group or individual wishes to reproduce information either in whole or in part from this book, please contact the authors first through the publishers.

Rapunzel's Revenge: Fairytales for Feminists
1. Short stories, English — Irish authors
2. Short stories, English — Women authors
3. Fiction, English — 20th Century
I. Title
823'.01'089287 FS PR8875

ISBN: 0-946211-18-3

First published in 1985 by:
Attic Press,
(in conjunction with
Women in Community Publishing Course 1984/85)
48 Fleet Street,
Dublin 2.

Typeset in 11pt Andover by Photo-set Limited.

Printed by Mount Salus Press Limited.

Editorial/Production: Anne Claffey, Linda Kavanagh, Sue Russell.
Cover Design: Siobhan Condon.
Illustrations: Siobhan Condon, Wendy Shea.

The fairies gratefully acknowledge the assistance of the following: Patsy Murphy, our fairy godmother; Irish Feminist Information, (Fairy Roisin and Fairy Mary Paul) for their constant help and harrassment and all the women on the Women in Community Publishing Course 1984/85 who brainstormed this book into existence.

CONTENTS

The Princesses' Forum

ONCE upon a time, all the princesses and heroines of fairy tales got together at Snow White's cottage to discuss the shortage of intelligent princes.

'I've decided that there's no point in hanging around my place, waiting for some idiot to force his way through the thicket,' said the Sleeping Beauty (who was really quite wide awake).

'And *I'm* sick of that lunatic with the foot fetish,' said Cinderella. 'Imagine selecting your life partner on the basis of her shoe size? How could any self-respecting woman cope with a man like that?'

'After keeping house for the seven dwarfs,' said Snow White, 'I never want to see another man again. Not one of them ever put the cap back on the toothpaste or washed their smelly socks.'

'I know exactly what you mean,' said Rapunzel, 'The one who came courting me wasn't very bright. Can you imagine it? Being trapped at the top of a tower, unable to escape. I was delighted when this fellow climbed up — I was sure my days as a prisoner were over. But the fool climbed down again! Each time he came back, he promised to bring a ladder with him the next time. But he kept on forgetting.'

'Forgetting my foot,' said Cinderella (who had feet on the brain). 'I just hope for your sake that you're not in any trouble.'

'In trouble?' said Rapunzel, looking surprised. 'How could I be in trouble? Since the day when you all rescued me, I've been in great form. I'm eating like a horse and I've put on half a stone in weight —'.

'What—?' shrieked all the princesses and heroines in unison. 'Did you say "half a stone in weight?"'

'Yes,' said Rapunzel in happy innocence. 'But there's just one teeny weeny problem, which one of you might be able to advise me about. Lately, I always seem to feel queasy in the mornings—.'

She looked askance as the others fell about the place in consternation.

'To think that we got together to discuss the shortage of princes —' groaned Snow White.

'— and already, there's been one prince too many,' finished the Sleeping Beauty crossly.

'Well there's only one thing to do,' said Cinderella, 'and that is to take her to Red Riding Hood's grandmother in the forest. She's an expert in dealing with this kind of situation. I'll take her there immediately after this meeting.'

Rapunzel sat silently, bewildered at the response that had been generated by her comments. She made a mental note to keep quiet in future.

'Right,' said Snow White, bringing the meeting back to order. 'We were discussing the princes. Since the only ones available are an unimpressive lot, what are we going to do?'

'It's all very well for *you*,' piped up Goldilocks. 'I've *never* had a prince of my own. Being chased by three bears is no fun, you know. I'd prefer a boor to a bear any day.'

'I agree,' piped up Rapunzel, breaking her self-imposed rule of silence. 'I think . . . .'

'If I were you,' said Cinderella, looking directly at her, 'I'd keep my big mouth shut.'

'Order, order,' called Snow White. 'I repeat — what are we going to do?'

'I think we're all victims of stereotyping,' said Red Riding Hood. 'Everyone assumes that in order to live happily ever after, we must each have a prince in tow. Give me a fine specimen of wolfhood any day. Or a woodcutter,' she added, lowering her eyes and blushing happily at the recent memory.

'I don't see why we need to have princes at all,' said the Sleeping Beauty. 'I'm not particularly keen to have some idiot come along and try to annexe my territory to his, under the guise of having fallen madly in love with me.'

'But princesses *have* to marry, and it *has* to be a prince,' said Goldilocks. 'Otherwise, there'll be no heirs to the kingdom, and . . . .'

'*King*dom,' repeated Cinderella. 'Now *there's* a word I object to. Why shouldn't it be a Queendom?'

'I suppose it's like the word "man",' said Red Riding Hood. 'It's meant to cover both men and women.'

'Well, I for one, object to being called a man,' said the Sleeping Beauty. 'I don't even look like one, do I?'

'I'm tired of having to behave as princesses are supposed to behave,' said Snow White. 'I'm not delicate, I'm not silly and I'm certainly not weak. Anyone who could keep house for seven little chauvinists — and not lose their sanity — has to be a very strong person.'

'Have you noticed,' said the Sleeping Beauty suddenly, 'that in

many of our stories, our enemies are other women?'

'That's because men wrote the stories,' said Cinderella. 'It makes them feel good to have women fighting among themselves for male attention.'

'Well then,' said the Sleeping Beauty, 'we'll just have to re-write the stories ourselves. I'd just love to rescue some good-looking fellow who's been imprisoned in a castle or tower by a wicked uncle or step-father.'

'That's a ridiculous plot,' said Goldilocks contemptuously.

'I know,' said the Sleeping Beauty, 'but it's actually the plot of *our* stories in reverse.'

'I hope we're not just going to reverse the situation,' said Cinderella. 'In that event, we'd only be reversing the roles of oppressor and oppressed. I don't want to oppress anyone.'

All the women nodded in agreement.

'The first change *I* want to make,' said Snow White, 'is to get my stepmother the Queen on our side. Once we're not in competition for men's approval, it won't matter which of us is better-looking. Then she'll have no reason to be jealous of me anymore. Besides, she's a very brilliant woman, with her own laboratories downstairs in the castle dungeon. I'm sure I could convince her to develop the science of pharmacology for good rather than evil.'

'When you think of it,' said Cinderella, 'there will be no need for other women to be our enemies if we're not fighting over who gets those macho idiots. What fun we could all have together instead!'

At that precise moment (as always conveniently happens in fairytales) three princes arrived at the castle door. They had been on an ego trip through the forest, looking for dragons to fight or helpless princesses to rescue.

Seeing Cinderella peering down at them from one of the castle windows, their eyes lit up with delight. The first one gave an exaggerated bow and nearly fell off his horse. 'Hi there, gorgeous!' shouted the second one. 'Do you need to be rescued?' shouted the third one.

Cinderella's reply was certainly not the type of language normally attributed to demure princesses.

'Invite them in,' said Snow White, nudging her in the ribs. 'I think we should let them know that we're writing them out of the scripts.'

The princes looked bewildered as they were ushered into the room full of princesses and heroines. They were used to ogling females one at a time, but a whole room full of them was just too daunting a prospect.

Quickly, Cinderella explained the discussions that had taken place and the conclusions the women had reached. 'So you see,' she concluded, 'we're not very impressed with all that chest-beating macho stuff.'

The three princes looked from one to the other in astonishment. 'Do you mean that we don't need to be big, strong and fearless anymore?" asked the first one.

'Do you mean that princesses are *not* all frail and helpless?' asked the second one.

'Yes to both questions,' said Snow White. 'We're tired of behaving the way stereotyped princesses are supposed to behave. We're going to behave as *we* want from now on.'

Once again, the princes looked from one to the other, mopping their brows in unison. 'Phew,' said the first one.

'What a relief!' said the second one.

'That's the best news I've ever heard,' said the third prince. 'I'm tired of always feeling under pressure to be brave and fearless. I get awfully scared sometimes, but I've never been able to tell anyone else. I thought I was the only man who ever felt that way.'

The second prince said 'It's such a relief to be able to act naturally. I was terrified at the thought of having to battle my way through those enormous briars round the Sleeping Beauty's castle. Do you really mean that I don't have to do that anymore?'

'Definitely not,' said the Sleeping Beauty. 'You can call to the door, like any normal civilised visitor — as soon as I get all those briars cleared away, and get the palace cleaned up.'

'Let's all come round to your place next week,' said Goldilocks. 'Together, we could have the job done in an afternoon.'

Everyone nodded in agreement, including the three princes.

Meanwhile, Cinderella had managed to sit down beside the second prince. 'I think you're cute!' she whispered, I wouldn't mind writing *you* into my new script.'

The prince turned scarlet, but looked very pleased nevertheless. 'I wouldn't mind either,' he said timidly.

Just then, there was a loud hammering on the castle door, and another prince — carrying a ladder — was ushered into the room. His initial bewilderment gave way to delight when he saw Rapunzel. 'Darling!' he cried.

'Precious!' she answered, and they rushed into each others' arms.

'I was really worried . . .' murmured the prince '. . . when you weren't in the tower. I'd planned *such* a romantic escape.'

9

'Well,' said Snow White, 'at least he's had the decency to turn up.'

'Do you realise,' said Cinderella, tapping him on the shoulder, 'that you've got this poor creature pregnant?'

Rapunzel and her prince both looked astonished.

'But I thought . . .' began the prince.

'What on earth do you mean?' asked Rapunzel angrily. 'I think you've got a nerve.'

'Well,' said Snow White, 'you said yourself that you've put on half a stone in weight.'

'That's because I've been taking the pill,' said Rapunzel crossly. 'You don't think we'd start a deep, meaningful relationship without being responsible about it?'

The gathering of princesses and heroines gave an audible sigh of relief.

Just then the door creaked open, and a snout with large gleaming fangs appeared. Cinderella pulled open the door, and a large hairy wolf fell into their midst.

'What on earth are you doing here?' said Red Riding Hood crossly.

'Sorry,' said the wolf, rising to his feet. 'I was just looking for someone to eat. It's way past dinner time, and I'm absolutely starving.'

'Look here,' said Cinderella, 'this kind of carry-on just isn't acceptable any more. We've decided to re-write all the fairy tales, and if you're not going to behave civilly, we'll write you out of the Red Riding Hood story altogether.'

'Oh please don't do that,' said the wolf miserably. 'I only eat people because I can't afford to buy food. Wealthy people like yourselves never give a thought to the plight of us poor.'

The group was silent for a moment, then Cinderella spoke. 'Perhaps we could remedy the situation, by having some kind of regular payment for those who don't earn enough to live on,' she said turning to the wolf. 'Will you promise to give up eating people, if this can be arranged?'

'Wolf's honour,' said the wolf, holding up his right forepaw. 'Quite honestly, I prefer the tinned or frozen stuff. People tend to give me indigestion anyway . . . .'

The group rose to its feet, and everyone began to prepare for their departure from the castle.

'I'm going home to have a serious talk with my stepsisters,' said Cinderella to Goldilocks, as she put on her cloak. 'I did an assertiveness training course recently, and I learned how to stand up for myself in the face of those two bullies. *My* days of being tied to the kitchen sink are definitely over.'

'Good for you,' said Goldilocks approvingly, 'and please tell me where you did the course. I think *I* need something like that to deal with those three aggressive bears.'

Outside the castle, the Sleeping Beauty was sitting astride her horse. 'Are you fellows okay?' she asked looking down at the three rather forlorn-looking princes, who were standing — typically — apart from the women.

'Of course,' replied the first prince, puffing out his chest. Then he remembered what had transpired at the meeting. 'Well — er — no, actually,' he confessed. 'To be perfectly honest — now that we're all going to be honest with each other, that is — I'm really quite frightened at the thought of going home alone through the dark forest.' The other two princes nodded in assent.

'Don't worry,' said the Sleeping Beauty. 'I'm passing your palaces on my way home. You'll be quite safe with me.'

'Besides,' added Snow White, from the castle doorway, 'there'll be nothing to be afraid of any more, if the wolf, the witches and the dragons are all our friends.'

Cinderella approached the second prince. 'If you're worried about going home alone —' she whispered, 'I'll go with you and hold your hand.'

The second prince and Cinderella disappeared into the woods together.

'Goodbye everyone,' called Goldilocks and Red Riding Hood, as they headed off together down the woodland path.

'Don't forget,' the Sleeping Beauty called after them,' my place next week! When the briars are cleared away, we'll all have a sing-song and a few bottles of wine. Is everyone agreed?'

'Sounds great,' said the first prince.

'Have you any whisky?' asked the third prince hopefully.

The wolf was too busy feasting — at Snow White's table — to reply. But he did manage to grunt in agreement.

Rapunzel and her prince smiled dreamily in assent, hardly able to think of anything but each other.

When they had all gone home, Snow White closed the castle door, and headed downstairs to her stepmother's laboratory. Perhaps, she thought, they *would* all live happily ever after.

Linda Kavanagh

Goldilocks Finds a Home

ONCE upon a time in happy-ever-after land, deep in the Concrete Jungle lived three bears. It was a typical nuclear family, Papa Bear, Mama Bear and the obligatory Baby Bear. With Papa Bear an upwardly mobile young executive type, they lacked none of the material comforts of a middle-class bear life. Their architect-designed solar-powered house nestled in neo-Georgian splendour amidst the trees, while their smaller, more compact town house was located in an up market corner of Disenchantment Wood. Papa's pride and joy — his latest model Toyota — nestled in the double garage beside Mama Bear's utilitarian but immaculate Mini. The kitchen was a Mama Bear's dream, with all the latest appliances, updated annually. Baby Bear's room was decorated as current trends dictated — plenty of high-tech, educational, non-sexist toys.

However, amid all this comfort and convenience the Bears were careful not to neglect their social responsibilities. Papa Bear was a prominent member of his local Clean Street Campaign and consistently maintained his annual subscription to *Save the World Monthly* magazine. Mama Bear dedicated two nights a week to various left-of-centre, but socially acceptable groups. The 'Land Rights for Gay Whales' and 'Vegies for All' movements were typical examples, and Mama Bear could organise a sit-in, phone-in or fast-in at the drop of a hat.

It must be said at this point that Mama Bear was always very careful not to neglect her family amidst all this activity. To Baby Bear, she devoted one hour each day of intensive one-to-one interaction (whether Baby Bear felt like it or not). This, she felt, was what every bear needs, just as important as a healthy diet and stimulating lifestyle.

Every morning the three Bears, Papa Bear, Mama Bear and the barely conscious Baby Bear left the house for their two kilometre jog through the forest. Before leaving the house, Mama Bear would prepare her 'special recipe' apple juice made from her own organically grown apples, and lay out a delicious bowl of sugar-free muesli ready for their return.

And so it happened that one fine June morning while they were out for their usual morning run, the lives of the three Bears were to be unalterably changed by circumstances beyond their control.

In another part of the Concrete Jungle someone else was out walking, but for a very different reason. Goldilocks (so called, since a freak accident with a bottle of peroxide) McCarthy was out for a walk to try to clear her head. Life in the last few months had been a nightmare for Goldilocks as she helped her mother to plan their escape. Home had become a prison with her father the gaoler. His had been a prison of the mind, he was too clever to use force. Bruises on the outside were easily seen, but mental scars were harder to see and harder to heal. They had thought it just a sign of the times at first — a tightening of the belt, watching the pennies to mind the pounds. But soon it was not just money that had to be accounted for, but time as well. It had been horrible to watch him tightening his grip, taking complete control of everything and everyone around him — her time, her money, her life.

It had taken all her mother's resources to pack her bags, leave, take the children and go. Go where? That was the question. Where does a 'happily married woman' with three children and no money go? Staying with Aunt Liz was fine for now, but they were living on top of each other and sooner or later he would find them out.

Goldilocks trudged on, deeper into the Concrete Jungle tired, hungry and worn out from worry. Walking along with her head down she was nearly run over by a family of enthusiastic joggers. That's funny, she thought, I didn't know that there were bears living this far out. But she dismissed them from her mind and walked on. Try as she could, Goldilocks could not see a solution to her problem and was just about to turn back home, when suddenly in a clearing just ahead she caught a glimpse of a magnificent house.

The first thing Goldilocks noticed about it was the garden. It was a children's wonderland. Every conceivable kind of toy was there, swings, roundabouts, climbing frames, slides, the lot. Enough to keep twenty children occupied. But where were the children? There wasn't sign or light of anyone around the place and everything looked brand new. Goldilocks couldn't resist a quick go on the swings. She felt like a child again as she swung higher and higher. It had been a long time since she had let herself go like this. Better be careful, she thought, this swing won't take my weight for much longer, and indeed as she jumped off she saw that the seat was slightly bent. Oh well, she thought, at least it's been used.

Still puzzled by the lack of signs of life, Goldilocks drew nearer to the house. She had never been so close to such a large house before. The garage alone was probably as big as the house where she and her family were living at present. Looking quickly around, she decided to risk a quick peek through the window. She could not believe her eyes. In the middle of the most perfect kitchen, with gleaming equipment and space enough to feed an army, was a table laid for breakfast — for three people! With hunger rumbling in her stomach she could almost taste the food and smell the coffee which was bubbling away on the hob. Before she could make a move however, she heard footsteps approaching through the forest. Quickly she jumped down and took cover behind the sandpit determined to see who lived there.

It was Baby Bear who noticed something amiss as he returned from his run.

'Someone's been swinging on my swing,' he said, 'and it's all bent. Look.'

'Don't be silly,' said Mama Bear. 'There's no one around here for miles. Now come inside and eat your breakfast, there's a good boy.'

Being a well brought up little bear he did as he was told.

*   *   *

As she made her way back home, Goldilocks pondered life's injustices. To think of her mother, herself and two children all crowded into Aunt Liz's tiny house while those three bears were rattling around in that huge house. More than ever she determined to do something to change the situation.

First, she sought help from the local Concrete Jungle Housing Bureau. The waiting list for houses was endless. The bear in charge was totally unsympathetic and suggested to Goldilocks that she and her mother go back home like 'good little girls' and not cause trouble. Looking around the office, it seemed to Goldilocks that this was the general advice given to women in that situation. Most of them looked tired and weary and ready to give up. A roof over their heads, a bite to eat and somewhere for the children to play — it's little enough to ask, thought Goldilocks . . . Somewhere for the children to play . . . Suddenly it hit her . . . I know where there's a place for our family and a few more besides. Now if only . . .

Goldilocks drew up a plan of action. She watched the three Bears' house every morning for a week and saw that they never changed their routine. Once or twice she even went inside and tasted the food and checked out the number of bedrooms. Baby Bear seemed to be the only one who noticed. Mama and Papa Bear were oblivious and paid no attention to Baby Bear's remarks about missing bowls of muesli. Maybe they just don't know what's going on out here in the Jungle, thought Goldilocks. They musn't realise how different things are for the rest of us.

She contacted her local Housing Action Group as well as her women's group and talked to them about her plan. It was quite straightforward as far as she could see. The three bears had two houses, both of which were far too big for their own needs — she and the others had no house at all. So? . . .

The plan was simple. Goldilocks, her mother and sisters and two other homeless single mothers would install themselves in the house while the three bears were out running through the forest. They would offer the bears a choice — they could either move into their town house in Disenchantment Wood or they could all live together as a community. Goldilocks' mother expressed doubts about living with the Bears. She hadn't got out of the frying pan only to leap into the fire. But Goldilocks assured her that the Bears were quite harmless really, and would possibly be taken with the idea of a commune.

*　　*　　*

And so it happened. The plan worked like a dream. On the appointed day the three Bears went jogging quite unawares. In went Goldilocks and friends. They prepared to blockade the doors in case the Bears got nasty and called on the Grizzlies. But they need not have worried. Although slightly take aback at having their home taken over, Mama Bear and Papa Bear took it pretty well. When Papa expressed a little dismay at having to move the Toyota to make room in the garage for extra storage space, Mama was quick to remind him of the article in last month's *Planet Savers Today* about communes. It would be quite an experience to actually live in a *real* commune instead of just reading about it. And anyway, she whispered, we can always go to the town house if things get a bit much here.

Baby Bear remained the only fly in the ointment. He was absolutely horrified at the idea of having to share his toys and space. He threw a huge tantrum, until Mama Bear — totally perplexed at his behaviour — actually shouted at him to stop. Baby Bear got such a shock that he stopped in his tracks, speechless. He too began to see that things would never be the same again down in the woods.

Sue Russell

Jack's Mother and The Beanstalk

'AH WELL, you have to speculate to accumulate,' sighed Jack's mother when Jack came home with the bag of beans. 'That's the first rule in business.'

She wondered sometimes whether it was wise to try to teach Jack the rudiments of business administration. It seemed to confuse him and gave him headaches. More in hope than in anticipation she planted the beans outside their little cottage and went back to reading the *Financial Times*.

All night the beanstalk grew until in the morning it reached the sky.

'Keep my dinner warm in the oven, Jack,' Jack's mother, said putting on a pair of her dead husband's breeches before starting her climb up the beanstalk.

'MOTHER!' screeched Jack when he saw her. 'You can't go out dressed like that. What'll the neighbours think?'

'We don't have any neighbours,' Jack's mother said and continued to climb.

When she reached the top of the beanstalk she found herself on a path that led eventually to a tall castle. Tired and hungry she let herself in and helped herself to some soup that was bubbling on the stove. Afterwards she fell asleep in a cupboard.

When she awoke it was dark. She peeped out through a crack in the door. At the table sat an enormous giant who was shovelling food into his mouth. He looked vaguely familiar but she could not think why. Suddenly he stopped eating and sniffed loudly. In a voice that made the castle shake he roared:

> *'Fee fi fo fum*
> *I smell the blood of an Englishman*
> *Be he alive or be he dead*
> *I'll grind his bones to make my bread.'*

'Well, that's the limit!' thought Jack's mother and leapt out of her hiding place. 'It's one thing calling me English. I could forgive that,' she shouted, boxing the giant hard on the ears. 'But it's another thing to say that I smell like a man, you male chauvinist giant.' She gave him an

almighty punch on the nose.

'That's not fair,' he shouted back.

'Yes it is,' she snarled.

'No it isn't. I've never discriminated,' the giant said in an injured tone. 'Man or woman, I'll eat either.'

The giant and Jack's mother glared at each other and then the giant began to chase her around the table but she was too quick for him. She led him through the castle, up and down stairs, in and out of rooms until the giant collapsed into a chair clutching his chest. (He had a weak heart — the result of too much protein in his diet. Eating people isn't just wrong, dear reader, it's also bad for your health.) She climbed onto a window ledge and looked at him closely.

Finally she spoke: 'I know you. You came into my office when I worked as an investment consultant before I married that good-for-nothing farmer. You ran a business — Giant Inc. I even invested in it myself. Two grand I put in and then you did a bunk. You lowdown, lily-livered rat!' She looked around the room. 'You did alright for yourself though I'll say that for you. Lovely pad you've got. A quick inventory and I'll tell you how much you're worth.'

Jack's mother took out a notebook and began to write. 'Nice work, giant,' she complimented him when she had totted up the figures.

'You've got some good antiques. Great pictures too. Originals. I like them. Now I'll work out my percentage and take my cut.'

'But I'm a *giant*,' wailed the giant. 'From me you're supposed to flee in fear.'

'From me you get a flea in your ear,' Jack's mother snapped back. 'Keep quiet, I'm calculating.' To show she meant business she dug her biro between his ribs. The giant groaned and covered his eyes.

'Taking interest into account,' Jack's mother continued, 'plus accumulated profit I reckon you owe me nine million, fourteen thousand, three hundred and twenty five pounds. Seeing as you're an old friend I'll leave off the twenty five pounds.'

The giant breathed heavily. He seemed to be recovering his strength. Quickly Jack's mother surveyed the room. Her attention was caught by the sight of a hen that was sitting on a clutch of golden eggs. 'Now there's a good investment,' she said admiringly as she scooped the hen into her arms. 'I'll take her as part payment.'

In the corner a magical harp was playing mournfully to itself.

'I adore music,' said Jack's mother.'I'll take the harp as the rest of the payment.'

'Oh heaven,' twanged the harp gratefully as Jack's mother escaped out the door, the harp in one hand, the hen in the other. 'At last, I've someone who appreciates me. You can't imagine what hell it's been living with that giant. All he ever listens to is James Last and Barry Manilow.'

Jack's mother was too busy running down the path to reply. With the giant in hot pursuit she began to climb down the beanstalk. 'Get the axe!' she hollered to Jack. 'This is an example of asset-stripping,' she informed him as womanfully she swung the axe at the beanstalk. Within seconds the beanstalk came crashing down around them. 'Chop it up,' she instructed Jack handing him the axe. 'We'll sell the pieces for firewood. We won't make much on it but no venture is too small — that's the second rule of business, Jack.'

Thanks to the hen that laid the golden eggs, the magical harp and Jack's mother's business acumen, Jack and his mother lived happily and prosperously ever after.

Jack never got the hang of business administration but then he didn't need to!

Elizabeth O'Driscoll

FEMINIST WORD SEARCH

Find the words. Move up, down, across or diagonally. All you need is a pencil — and your feminist consiousness!

```
Q  H  Y  G  L  A  M  O  U  R  R  T  H
Y  G  L  A  Y  H  M  T  I  F  T  A  S
H  Q  T  S  I  N  I  M  E  F  R  I  P
C  H  I  G  C  R  O  N  F  P  S  L  I
R  H  E  O  A  N  D  C  I  S  P  I  N
A  C  I  L  I  H  P  O  I  B  E  A  S
I  T  R  I  V  I  A  F  L  D  E  P  T
R  I  L  M  S  I  C  R  O  X  E  O  E
T  W  A  C  O  I  R  V  I  R  T  R  R
A  B  E  G  A  Y  O  V  E  N  T  C  L
P  A  T  R  I  A  N  O  W  H  U  E  N
J  D  O  O  H  R  E  T  S  I  S  N  Y
```

For solution to word search send stamped addressed envelope to Attic Press, 48, Fleet St., Dublin 2.

Biophilic	Sisterhood	Spinster
Crone	Hag	Witch
Exorcism	Necrophilia	Trivia
Feminist	Patriarchy	Voyage
Glamour	Gynocide	Suttee

The Plastic Princess

ONCE upon a time, in a ramshackle palace on the edge of a forest, there lived a king and queen. A very strange place for a king and queen to live, you might say, but they had been deposed by a popular uprising in their country and had barely escaped with their lives and treasures. In a fit of nostalgia, the king had spent most of the contents of his treasure trove on building a replica of the palace in which they had lived. Unfortunately the only available place was the edge of a forest. Another problem was that so much of the king's treasure trove had been eaten up by the building of the palace, that he did not have enough to pay for repairs over the years. The result was a ramshackle palace on the edge of a forest.

The queen refused to lend the king any money from her personal treasure. She had not approved of his extravagance in building a palace. Sensible woman that she was, she would have been satisfied to live in a semi somewhere more accessible than a forest. So inconvenient for shops and socialising, she thought. Of course, men never think of things like that.

The queen would have had a lonely life, since the king spent most of his time in the counting house, had she not been accompanied in her flight from her queendom by a group of fairies. Now, the queen and her twelve friends spent their days in an endless round of tea, light household duties, needlepoint and consciousness raising. It was at one of these consciousness raising sessions that the queen announced that she was pregnant. The fairies were delighted at the news and they talked about the future princess. They were sure it would be a princess and often discussed among themselves the kind of qualities she would need to cope with living in such straitened circumstances as had befallen the royal family.

The queen gave birth to a baby girl in due course. The delighted queen sent out invitations to all who lived in the forest to come to a banquet to celebrate the birth. It was an occasion of great rejoicing and all twelve fairies were dressed in their finest gossamer and lace. After the feasting the fairies proceeded to confer their gifts on the princess.

21

One wished her a flair for mathematics and technology.

Another wished her assertiveness and audacity.

A third wished her strength and a sound head for business.

By the time they had finished, the princess had been granted a range of gifts that would ensure that she would grow up strong, independent and free.

'Wait,' a voice came from the assembled crowd, 'you have not yet heard *my* gift.'

The king and queen were surprised when a woman stepped forward from the crowd. She was a small woman, as broad as she was high, dressed in black from head to foot and positively bristling with anger.

'Who are you?' asked the queen who was more than a little amused at this unexpected visitor's appearance.

'Who am I indeed,' replied the little woman. 'I am your fairy godmother and you did not even think to invite me to your banquet. Instead you invited this bunch of flibbertigibbets.' She angrily indicated the other fairies. 'Assertiveness, business head, mathematics, whoever heard of such gifts for a princess? Would you have got where you are today if I had given you those gifts instead of beauty, grace, meekness, and the ability to do fine needlework.'

'Beauty, grace, meekness and the ability to do fine needlework were all very well when I led a life of luxury and idleness,' replied the queen, 'but times have changed. I don't want my daughter to live the rest of her life on the edge of a forest.'

'That's just what she will do without beauty, grace and the qualities that will attract a prince,' said the old fairy. 'My gift to the princess is that at the age of fifteen, she will fall in love with a handsome prince and live happily ever after.'

With these words, the old fairy left the palace in a cloud of dust. When the shock of her words had subsided, people began to leave the palace thanking the queen for her hospitality.

'Happily ever after,' the queen muttered tearfully, 'that's what they wished me when I was young.'

'I know,' the other fairies said gloomily, 'we all know what that means.'

'Poor little thing!' another fairy looked at the sleeping princess. They thought of the long days of boredom the queen had endured while her husband was in the counting house, of the drudgery of household chores, the tedium of having to be a submissive, dutiful wife, the pointlessness of needlepoint.

'I haven't given my gift yet,' said the youngest fairy crawling from beneath the drinks table. 'I'm afraid I passed out after my fourteenth vodka. I cannot take away the spell but I *can* do something to lessen its effects. The princess will not live happily ever after. She will endure ten years of happily married bliss and at the end of that time be delivered.'

The queen shed tears of relief and gratitude. The king could not understand what all the fuss was about and slipped away to the counting house.

The princess grew up in an environment that was happy, frugal and female. Before her second birthday, the king died of lead poisoning contracted by handling old coins. In order to avert the curse of the happy ever after, the queen decided to educate the princess at home with only women tutors and girls as playmates. Thus the princess reached the age of fifteen without ever having seen a member of the opposite sex — except of course, for the old king who remained a dimly remembered figure from the past. Despite the queen's attempts to protect her daughter, rumours had spread beyond the bounds of the forest of the clever, assertive princess. A prince from a far kingdom, tired of the beautiful but boring princesses from whom his parents wished him to select a bride, heard of her and set off to try to make her his wife.

*   *   *

It was the princess' fifteenth birthday. She had opened all her presents, put on her new birthday dungarees, spiked her hair but still she was not satisfied. Something was missing from her life. She had a comfortable, if ramshackle, home. She was surrounded by loving females, both human and fairy.

She was the greatest mathematical genius the forest had ever known. Strong and assertive, she always got her own way in arguments and games. Why then was she dissatisfied? The fact was, the princess was bored. So after breakfast, she decided that she would explore a corner of the forest that she had never entered before. She slipped away from those rather tiresome fairies who had been with her for as long as she could remember and set off.

The forest was dark and deep and quiet. The princess discovered for the first time the pleasure of being alone. As she ran through a long, cool grove the leaves rustling beneath her feet, she heard a cry of 'Who goes there?' The princess stopped. That voice was deeper than

any she had heard before. She stepped forward cautiously and soon came face to face with a being who, though recognisably human, was unlike anyone the princess had ever seen. It was taller and had a different shape from anyone she had known before. Its auburn hair hung to its shoulders and, most interesting to the princess, its upper lip sprouted a luxuriant crop of hair.

'Who are you?' asked the princess.

'I am Prince Florizel,' he replied, a little taken aback at being spoken to first by a woman.

'I'm Princess Alicia and I've never met a prince before.'

The young people were enchanted with each other. The prince had never met such a young woman before. She did not wait to be spoken to and was not slow to argue her points with the prince. They forgot the time as they sat and talked with each other so that in the palace, there was consternation about her whereabouts.

'How could I have been so careless?' the queen reproached herself. 'On her fifteenth birthday, of all the days to leave her unattended. She could even have met a man by now.'

When she came home, the princess was reluctant to talk about where she had been but the queen knew by her glazed eyes, her general air of distractedness and the inane smile that settled on her face that she was in love. Within six months, the princess had married Prince Florizel and left the ramshackle palace in the forest to live in the stately house of her husband. In vain did her mother and the fairies point out the difficulties of marriage. In fact, the assertiveness that had been one of her greatest assets now worked against them as she insisted on a short engagement and a spring wedding.

*   *   *

So, the happily ever after began. Newspapers and magazines all over the world carried pictures and stories of the happy couple. Prince Florizel never appeared in public unaccompanied by his adoring wife. But there was a change in her appearance. She no longer spiked her hair. She exchanged her dungarees for elegant gowns, high heeled shoes that ensured she could take no more than mincing steps. She learned to preface everything she said with 'My husband and I . . . . ' The world watched her emerge year after year from the Royal Lying-In Hospital with another fragrant, white bundle. It was only when after the birth of her seventh child, it was announced in the *Daily Fable* that Prince Florizel had spent the time of his wife's confinement playing ludo with some wastrel friends of his, that the world began to suspect that the happily ever after was not as happy as it appeared. Further rumours suggested that the princess' serene appearance might owe more to tranquilizers than tranquility. The prince began to appear in public without his consort. She was only seen from a distance when she appeared on a balcony to wave mechanically to the adoring crowds who gathered at the palace hoping for a glimpse of the royals. The royal children were always accompanied by an entourage of nannies and nurse maids when they went out. More rumours appeared in the *Daily Fable*. This time it was alleged that the Princess was no longer living at the palace but had run away with one of her ladies in waiting to join a women's commune in a neighbouring country. What the people saw on the balcony of the palace was, in fact, a perfectly constructed model. The royal family vigorously denied such rumours. There was even a threat of a libel suit against the *Daily Fable*. This was all forgotten about when a rival newspaper, the *Elfish Echo* printed the true story of the princess' flight from the kingdom written by one of her ladies who had tired of waiting. 'The Plastic Princess' the headlines read. This time, the palace did not deny the rumours. When people heard that the princess had run away with her attendant, they were so outraged that they refused to believe it and the author of the rumours was threatened with such violence that she had to leave the country. The Prince continued to live in the palace with the Plastic Princess, who was indistinguishable from the real one. She smiled graciously from the balcony, waved elegantly to her admirers and continued to preface all her sayings with 'My husband and I . . . .'

*   *   *

And the real princess began to spike her hair again, stopped wearing high heeled shoes and devoted her energies to the commune for princesses who had outlived the 'happy ever after'.

Anne Claffey

All The Better To See You

THE EVENING BLURB lay on the floor open at page three. 'Grandmother Held Hostage — daring rescue by pretty young granddaughter' read the headline.

'The unexpected arrival of fifteen year old Rosa Hood put an end to Billy Wolf's plans to evade the police. Wolf (20) gained entry to the old woman's flat by a back window and was hiding there when Rosa arrived. Though tall for her age, Rosa is of slight build, certainly no match for the husky young man she encountered on entering her grandmother's kitchen. But her angelic features belie the cunning she showed on this occasion. Pretending she thought the intruder to be her cousin, Rosa gained his confidence and sufficient time to alert the neighbours.

Police promptly arrived and apprehended the youth who was wanted in connection with a raid on the local pork butchers.

Rosa, who does not normally visit her grandmother on Friday morning, stated that she was not at school because 'Me Mammy was getting me a lovely new red leather jacket and I decided to let me granny see it. Lucky I did.'

The old woman was reportedly under sedation following the ordeal, and was unavailable for comment. Doctors say she is fit and well considering her age.'

Granny Hood snorted with contempt and poured herself a glass of Guinness. 'Unavailable for comment, huh! Always the same. Give granny her bottle and shove her in the corner'.

'Will you have another small one Granny? You should see the new scooter Joey's gettin'! I'd love to get one but I can't afford it. Any chance of a loan." Butter me up and then sneak in the hook. Mean pack o' touchers the lot o' them. Look at sweet little Rosa. Big smile for the camera, swear she wouldn't know how to put a foot wrong!'

'Lucky I came around when I did. James Street, I could kill her. All very well for her she gets her picture in the paper. Everyone thinks what a great little girl Rosa is, prancing about in her red leathers getting Billy Wolf put behind bars. Poor oul Granny is left here alone as usual!

'Fit and well, the only wan who comes near me is Mrs White. If it
wasn't for her I could be left here rotting away. She's busy enough
herself with those seven lads o' hers. So I'm left here be the window
day in day out.

'"God, granny what good eyes you've got." I can tell you they're good
— considering my age and the things I do see. That day I saw it all. I saw
the guards picking on the lads and when I found Billy on the balcony I
let him slip in — to hide like. He was always nice enough young fellow
to me. Looked rough but kept a civil tongue in his head.

'But of course darling Rosa comes bargin' in and sounds the alarm. If
only I hadn't been in the loo at the time. God, before I knew where I
was, this place was swarming with big booted, red necked guards
clompin' all over the joint and haulin' poor Billy Wolf off to the clanger.

'Did anyone listen to me? Not a bit of it. "Shock," they said when I
tried to stop them. "Senile," they said when I tried to tell Rosa that she
should've minded her own business. Just an old woman's ramblings —
not worth listening to.

'That's the way. Things will be harder now. Some of the lads will think I got Billy put away deliberately and he'll not be able to tell them otherwise.

'When will I see Rosa again? Next day the humour takes her or when she's something else to show off. But by bingo when I see that Rosa Hood again, I'll give her a piece of my mind and tell her that if she's not interested in seeing her granny more often she can just stick to her own neck o' the woods and leave me in peace. There's life in me yet and I'll not be sedated into letting that shaver live happily ever after.'

Granny Hood drained her Guinness contentedly, shoved the *Evening Blurb* in the bin and went off to bed followed by her black cat. Sleep tight!

Carol Lanigan

Little Ms Muffet

Wendy Shea

Hi Ho, It's Off To Strike We Go!

THERE WAS once a young woman who was clever and kind, serious and witty. On top of all that her family was wildly wealthy. Her name was Margaret, which is a perfectly useful and easy name to have, but of course didn't the family have to give her nickname, in the manner of families? Since she was born on the night of a dreadful blizzard, somebody or other decided to call her 'Snow White', and one way or another, the name stuck although for most of the time the family just used 'Snow', as in 'Snow, your tea is ready!'.

Apart from this bit of foolishness, there was little in the world to trouble our Snow during the years of her childhood, which she spent playing and romping, reading and thinking and turning over new ideas, just like most clever, kind, serious and witty young women. All would have gone on blissfully forever, if it hadn't been for her mother.

'I'm fed up looking at you playing and romping and reading and thinking and turning over new ideas,' Snow's mother said to her one day. 'Why don't you get a job?'

'Oh, mother, you are wicked,' Snow sighed. 'Anyway, there are no jobs. There's a recession, as you know very well.'

'Just the same, it's time you did something. If you go on hanging around here, what's to become of you? First thing you know, the hall will be cluttered with handsome suitors looking for your hand in marriage, and the next thing you'll pick out one of them to fall in love with, and within a year and a day, you'll be well on the way to ending up like myself. Look how your father made his money. Manufacturing Magic Mirrors. Do you know what the secret of Magic Mirrors' success is? Behind every mirror is a sheet of rosy pink, and every woman who looks into one thinks she's the fairest of them all. Small good it does any of us, I can tell you. Looking at yourself in a rose-tinted mirror is worse than looking at the world through glasses of the same hue, my girl, and I want you to make something of yourself.'

'Hmm,' said Snow. 'But if you're restless, mother, why not take an AnCO re-training course for yourself? I'm sure there's something you could learn to do.'

After that, her mother sent her packing for cheek, and so it was that Snow White went off in search of her fortune, or at least, a job. But there was a recession, of course, and truth to tell, she couldn't find anything that suited her, which is why she finally ended up answering an ad for a housekeeper in a tiny mining village.

She was interviewed by seven short, gnarled men who had a long and tedious list of chores she was meant to do each day: washing, cooking, sweeping, making beds, and so on. It sounded dreadful and the wages were pretty poor. But Snow White took the job, all the time privately wondering why seven men couldn't share out the housework among themselves.

By the time she had finished her first week's work, Snow White had her answer. The seven small miners worked sixteen hours a day in the Prince Precious Jewel Mining Company, and were so exhausted at night that they could barely scoff down the lovely porridge she cooked for them.

'For pity's sake,' Snow White asked them when she had her wages on Friday night, 'haven't you ever heard of the trade union movement?'

'No,' said the little miner named Dopey. 'Tell us the story, Snow White.'

So Snow White told them all about capital and exploitation and unity being strength and free collective bargaining, and on Monday morning the seven miners marched into Mr Prince and demanded shorter working hours, meal breaks, a rise in wages and a pension plan. When they had made all their demands, Mr Prince of the Prince Precious Jewel Mining Company told them they could take a running jump at themselves, so they trooped back to Snow White.

'What will we do now?' asked the miner named Sleepy, stifling a yawn.

'We will go on strike,' said Snow White. 'That ought to wake things up around here.'

So Snow White organised the seven little miners into picketing shifts and got everyone stuck into painting slogans on posters such as 'Precious little from Precious Jewel' and 'Prince pays poorly.' For three days and three nights the seven miners took it in turn to picket the mines, and Snow White took the fellows who were off picket duty and gave them a crash course in washing, cooking, sweeping and so on. She had some plans of her own at this point, you see.

On the third night, Mr Prince met the seven little miners and said 'All right, all right, I'll discuss your demands. This strike is costing me a dragon's ransom in unmined rubies and emeralds and diamonds.' So

Snow White took the seven little miners aside and told them to put all their demands all over again, but add onto it that they wanted at least one more worker.

'In fact, better say two more workers,' she advised. 'And for that matter, name a higher wage increase than you will settle for, and a better pension plan than you are looking for, and ask for five meal breaks instead of three. Industrial relations are only human relations, and must be negotiated.'

Eventually, the miners and Mr Prince worked out a settlement, and not a minute too soon either, because the porridge pot was running dry. 'Great news,' Snow White said briskly when the miners came back with the jubilant information that they had won. 'Now there'll be enough money again for porridge. One of you had better go out and buy some, because as of this minute, I am applying for a job as a miner.'

Off she went to Mr Prince's office. Now, Mr Prince was a likeable enough fellow and was, for his own part kind and serious, occasionally witty and bright enough, but weighed down with a lot of prejudices.

'Don't be absurd,' he told Snow White. 'This is no sort of work for a girl.'

'Why not?' asked Snow White. 'I'm not afraid of the dark and I have done my share of digging during the days when I was playing and romping and all that.'

'But you are beautiful,' Mr Prince said, 'and everyone knows that the right place for a beautiful girl is in the reception office, so how about a nice desk job, meeting visitors to the Prince Precious Jewel Mining Company?'

'As for that, personal comments have no place in the workplace,' Snow White said. 'However, I'll consider the receptionist job provided, naturally, that the pay is the same as the male miners get.'

At that, Mr Prince knew he was defeated and meekly agreed to send Snow White down the mines. After all, he could always find some other pretty little girl to take the job in the front office. 'Oh, and by the way,' Snow White said as she left his office, 'my union is keeping a sharp eye out for underpaid female labour. We wouldn't hesitate to strike again on behalf of someone you hire for the front office, if you don't pay properly.'

So it was that Snow White took up her shovel and pick and went down the mines. She also took care to see that the Precious Jewel Miners' Union promptly affiliated to all the other unions on the mountain, and succeeded in being elected chief shop steward at the first meeting of the Mountainside Miners' Associated Unions. She set about negotiating with the bosses, ogres and princes on a wide range

33

of benefits. She won protective safety wear, paid holidays, a sick pay scheme, grievance and appointments procedures and a positive action programme for all females employed on the mountain. She saw to it that the different managements set up subsidised canteens so as to eliminate all that porridge stirring, and insisted on creches as a matter of principle, though they were not yet required. 'They will be,' she assured Mr Prince and the other bosses firmly.

One night Mr Prince approached Snow White and asked if she was possibly free for dinner. 'I have a proposal I'd like to make to you,' he said shyly.

'I'll have to clear it with the union committee first,' Snow White answered, 'but I don't think they will object.'

Mr Prince took her to the nicest restaurant on the mountainside and asked what she'd like to eat. 'Anything but bloody porridge,' Snow White said, scanning the menu. 'Let's see: what about terrine de

34

campagne, followed by tournadoes medici and dessert?'

'Certainly,' said Mr Prince, 'with a nice bottle of champagne to follow.'

The meal went beautifully up until the end, when Mr Prince decided to order just cheese and a bit of fruit for afters. Snow White, being a sensible woman, had apricot torte with almonds and was just tucking into it when Mr Prince bit into his apple, choked and fell into a swoon.

Well, this threw everyone into a nice tizzy, as you can imagine. 'A swoon, a swoon, and I can't remember the words of one decent spell,' the owner of the restaurant kept shouting. Other customers tried out spells they could recall, and one or two said a spell in jail is what fellows who drank that much deserved.

Snow White, however, considered the situation and picked Mr Prince up by the heels, bending one arm expertly underneath his knees in a hold she had learned in karate class. She delivered one swift karate blow between his shoulder blades and, lo and behold, out came the bit of apple.

'There y'are now, not a bother on you.' Snow White said when Mr Prince opened his eyes. 'I think we had better be getting home, though, just to be on the safe side. What was it you wanted to propose to me?'

Mr Prince gazed at her with admiration and respect. 'I wanted to propose that you become my partner,' he said softly.

Snow White dusted off his suit, put his plumed hat back on his head and signalled a passing white steed to carry them off in the night.

'Only on one condition,' she said.

'Anything,' Mr Prince replied, his voice trembling.

'It would have to be a workers' co-op, and the unions would have to support my membership on the board. I'm sure we could devise suitable structures. I'll have to take a look at the EEC directives. It's certainly worth considering, and I am very interested in industrial democracy. It's about time we began taking over. Lovely meal, wasn't it? Apart of course, from the apple.'

Mary Maher.

Rapunzel's Revenge

RAPUNZEL MURPHY was a woman of no means but much imagination. She had worked in many different jobs, but the tide of recession was high and ensured she remained flotsam in the sea of unemployment. She frequently pictured herself, jazz singer extraordinaire in one of Dublin's top music clubs, campaigner for civil rights among the downtrodden masses or helping her friend Pauline Hyland grow her own food, and investigate the healing powers of wild plants on her small holding in west Donegal.

Rapunzel was ruminating in this fashion one Thursday morning returning from her weekly excursion to the labour exchange when she was interrupted by a clean cut smartly dressed man in his twenties. Before she could gather her wits she found herself being invited to participate in a marketing exercise for a new Sunsoft shampoo for fifty pounds a day. With images of a holiday at Pauline's in Donegal flashing through her mind she willingly answered the man's questions on her age, family background and next of kin.

He seemed delighted to hear that she was an only child and that her nearest living relative was an aunt who lived in Australia. Commenting on her luxurious head of hair he told Rapunzel that she was just the sort of 'girl' they were looking for. Would she be free to come to the company office the following day? Would she be free? Her feet could not carry her quickly enough to telephone Pauline to relate the good news. To Rapunzel's surprise Pauline was less than enthusiastic.

'Fifty pounds a day for getting your hair washed? Sounds a bit fishy to me. I've a feeling that company has been involved in animal experimentation and chemical pollution of the rivers.'

'Well I'm sick of being broke for good causes. Fifty quid is fifty quid and it will mean that we can have a good weekend together down at your place.'

Rapunzel felt distinctly uncomfortable the next morning as the warm water trickled down the back of her neck. She was sitting in the plush 'product testing salon' having her hair shampooed with 'New Improved Sunsoft.' Rory Prince, marketing manager, who had greeted her that morning as she signed the consent forms was everything that she despised, sleek and well groomed, every inch the image maker.

'Every man will fall at your feet, my dear,' he said condescendingly, 'after you have used our Sunsoft.'

'Spare me this,' thought Rapunzel. 'The things I do for money!'

Sitting under the hair dryer Rapunzel felt a strange, tingling sensation all over her scalp. She hoped that she was not going to be allergic to this stuff. They had assured her that it was absolutely non-allergenic, but she did not trust that Rory Prince one bit.

After the third wash and blow dry she definitely felt peculiar. She had the sensation that she had more hair than she had started out with that morning. There were no mirrors in the 'salon' so she could not immediately check this out. Lunch was provided for her, and very nice it was too, but she got a few strange looks in the company canteen. When her hair fell into her soup for the fourth time she really began to get suspicious.

By four o'clock in the afternoon a controlled panic had broken out in the salon. White-coated lab technicians scurried about with bottles of strange smelling solution and whispered together in corners. Even the smooth mask of Rory Prince's face could not disguise his disquiet.

'Well, well, dear, this is proving to be a most interesting experiment indeed. We would like you to be our guest for the night so that we can monitor the results. We have a charming suite of rooms upstairs which you may use.'

'I'm sorry, but I can't possibly stay,' said Rapunzel, 'I've got a weight-lifting class tonight . . .'

Rory Prince curled his lip in distaste, before the suave veneer descended again. 'Well, I'm sorry too, my dear,' he said, 'but you should have read the small print in your contract. It states that you must stay until we consider that the tests are complete. Let's not have any unpleasantness, my dear.' He propelled her in the direction of the lift.

Despite the soft bed and the luxurious surroundings of the suite, Rapunzel realised that she was a prisoner. There was no telephone in the room, no writing materials and Prince had locked the door behind him as he left. Tossing and turning on the bed with great difficulty as her hair was now down to her knees, Rapunzel wished she had listened to Pauline's doubts.

'I might have known that any company that polluted the rivers, and didn't care about bunny rabbits wouldn't care about people either.'

At the organic smallholders' group Pauline made enquiries about Sunsoft Beauty Products and heard there was a rumour they had closed a factory some years before when they were threatened with a public enquiry over serious environmental pollution. It was said too, they had strange links with a covert mercenary organisation in central Africa! Pauline grew uneasy when Rapunzel failed to arrive on Friday night as planned. By the next evening she began to be alarmed. Rapunzel might be weight training, but she was no heavyweight when it came to dealing with multinational corporations. Still it was a bit rich of her not to contact Pauline. On Tuesday morning she boarded the bus trying to suppress the rising anger and anxiety.

Rapunzel clambered around the growing mass of tangled hair. By this stage — had she really been here for five days — she sat five feet off the ground in one corner of the room, singing quietly to herself. Beside the door were stacked dozens of black plastic sacks full of hair. Two sour faced attendants were employed full time shearing away at the ever growing substance that was once her dead mother's pride and joy. The tight lipped calmness of Rory Prince and his entourage reinforced her belief that she was quite mad. Sister Angela's warnings about the evils of money echoed in her head. Maybe she would smother herself quietly in her sleep. Edward the tea boy was becoming quite agile on the step ladder by this stage. He was even mildly friendly. From her perch Rapunzel could see down into the street below, people living normal everyday lives, dole queues, racing ambulances, joy riding, and a lively demonstration in support of Sticky Nelly. She decided she would employ her time positively. Yes, that was it. She would systematically go through all her favourite composers . . . Cole Porter, Irving Berlin, Peggy Seeger, Holly Near, that was it! At least she could get at them with a few good feminist songs.

Pauline's conversation with Rapunzel's neighbour scared her. Not a sign of her for five days. It was near finishing time when she reached Sunsoft Beauty Products Ltd. No, they had never heard of anyone of the name Rapunzel Murphy. Perhaps if she came back tomorrow she could see the personnel manager. Pauline pushed her way through the tired workers as they emptied out of the lift. She swiftly worked her way through the maze of corridors. First floor, second floor. God, what an awful place to earn your living in, she thought. On the seventh floor she narrowly avoided two security guards dressed in uniforms.

'Has Mr. Snarl arrived yet?' one of them asked. 'Prince and Smarm and the other directors are waiting in the boardroom for him to begin an emergency sitting of the board to assess the situation.'

Pauline slipped quickly into the fire stairs entrance. I must be near the top of the building, she thought. This is ridiculous. What am I doing here? I'll go to the police. I'll ring the Samaritans. I'll go to the Women's Centre! God it's so dry and hot. What the hell was that other sound?

'I'm a woman. W-O-M-A-N. Du be du du.' Rapunzel! Two steps at a time is not fast enough, she thought as she raced upstairs, through the next fire doors and into a plush, pink coloured corridor lined with large refuse sacks. There was an over-powering smell of sweet synthetic soap. Rapunzel's voice was rising to a wild crescendo ... 'W-O-M-A-N AND THAT'S ALL. DU BE DU.'

'She's drunk ... or drugged. She's gone over the top this time. Oh God! She was always too bloody artistic. This damned city!'

Pauline tried the door. It was locked. 'Rapunzel,' she whispered. No answer came! 'Rapunzel,' she screamed. A door at the far end of the corridor opened and a thin, ashen faced youth appeared with a tray. Pauline ducked around the corner and watched. He slowly opened the door as the first verse of the *Union Maid* started. As the door closed behind him Pauline made a lurch at it sending youth, cups, plates, hamburger and chips flying into the centre of the room.

'My God, Rapunzel, what have they done to you?' gasped Pauline pushing her way through the mountains of hair. Shaking her head in disbelief, Pauline listened as Rapunzel revealed the horror of her ordeal over the last few days at the hands of Prince and his board of directors. Pauline's mind was working overtime — how to escape, how to expose the company for what they were. She looked at the snivelling Edward, who was pathetically fiddling with the hair surrounding him and suddenly she knew what to do.

'How long do these board meetings last?' she asked Edward, as she helped him up off the floor.

'Er, um, two or three hours at least,' he said.

'Good,' said Pauline, 'that gives us some time. Now, Rapunzel, you did that advanced weaving course last year. Do you think we could weave a web out of all this hair?'

'Well I suppose I could, but I don't see . . .'

'Never mind, just get cracking. Edward, can you help?'

'Yeah, sure, whatever you say,' said Edward dusting himself off.

'Right then, I'm going to find a phone and ring all the newspapers and the television as well and tell them to be here at eight o'clock for an urgent press conference. You stay here, Edward, and do what Rapunzel tells you. She'll teach you how to weave and you can help us to get out of here.'

'But what about my hair?' cried Rapunzel. 'They've tried everything to stop it and it's growing faster every day.'

'You leave that to me,' said Pauline tapping the pocket of her jeans. 'I haven't spent the last two years working with herbs for nothing. Once we have the media here, I'll cut your hair and we'll apply some of my oil of herbina which is so pure and uncontaminated it will counteract the effect of all those chemicals.'

Pauline dashed off to contact the press. Rapunzel began to teach Edward and, despite his clumsy fingers, they soon had a large and growing web flowing from their fingers. Pauline returned, her face flushed with excitement. 'They're on their way,' she assured Rapunzel, 'and the television cameras will be here as well.'

'Great,' said Rapunzel tying off the last of the knots in the web. Folding it carefully, she gave one end of it to Pauline and the other to Edward. They set off for the board room with Rapunzel managing as best as she could with five feet of hair trailing behind her. Quickly and quietly they ran down the fire stairs till they got to the seventh floor.

'Right, Edward, slip out there and check that the coast is clear,' instructed Pauline. 'Are you all right, Rapunzel?'

'Yes', puffed Rapunzel, slightly out of breath. 'I'm glad I took up weight lifting this year. This hair weighs a ton.'

'It won't be long now,' smiled Pauline. 'You'll soon have your revenge.'

'All clear,' whispered Edward. 'They're too busy arguing in there to hear a thing out here.'

'Just as well,' said Rapunzel as the lift doors opened. 'Here comes the press.'

'Okay, here we go,' said Pauline, 'you all know what to do.'

As they crept nearer to the boardroom, they could hear the directors' voices.

'If this gets out, we could be ruined!' said one voice, 'I don't see that we have any any other option.'

'I agree,' said another voice. 'We'll just have to get rid of her. It shouldn't be any problem. Don't forget, we picked a guinea pig without any nosey relatives.'

'I presume —' said another voice, '— that this will be one of our usual 'accidents?'

'Good God no!' said a harsh voice. 'We can't even risk *that*. She will simply have to — er! — disappear.'

This comment was followed by murmurs of approval.

Suddenly all was confusion. Rapunzel, Pauline and Edward burst into the room with the press hot on their heels. Before the startled board members could move, Rapunzel and Pauline flung the golden web over their astonished heads. With a flourish the two women turned to the assembled journalists.

'Here you have them, trapped in a web of their own making. This is the scoop of a lifetime, it's up to you to make sure they don't squirm out of this one.'

With that, Pauline turned to her friend and said 'What about that trip to Donegal? I think we deserve it after this.'

Anne Claffey
Roisin Conroy
Linda Kavanagh
Mary Paul Keane
Catherine MacConville
Sue Russell

The Sleeping Beauty wakes up to the Facts of Life

AURORA lay on the drawing-room couch with her eyes closed and thought about what the doctor had told her. She wanted to get everything sorted out in her mind before Desie got home for his tea.

It had all been a bit of a shock in a way, though she supposed she should have been prepared for it. After all, it was nearly a year since the wedding and the great ball at the Castle which followed it.

These things happened, she knew, although her mother had never quite explained how. But then her mother always had so many functions to attend and so much protocol to observe that she never had a great deal of time to spend with her daughter. It was one of the disadvantages of being a queen.

Maybe her mother would have explained it all to her if nothing had happened. Aurora remembered now that she had said on the morning of her sixteenth birthday that it was high time the two of them had a little talk. In fact, it was really because she had time on her hands before going to her mother's room at the appointed hour that she had started to explore the little room at the top of the turret. Aurora shuddered at the thought of it. That awful old woman in the black cloak and conical hat! But she had been so friendly at the time.

'After all,' she had said to Aurora, 'you're sixteen now. Don't you think, my dear, that it's time to savour life a little more fully? You've been kept from experiencing so much. You really ought to try everything at least once.'

As it happened, that was much the way Aurora herself had been feeling at the time. Being a princess, she thought, was almost as bad as being a prisoner: always confined to the palace grounds and only able to read the books her teachers thought suitable and meet the people her parents approved of.

And then her parents began to talk about finding her a suitable husband. It was not fair, Aurora thought, for them to want to organize something so important to her without first giving her a chance to meet boys of her own age from outside the court, and perhaps even choose a husband for herself. She was feeling thoroughly rebellious so, when the old woman had said she could arrange a trip for Aurora too, she had not hesitated for long.

'Everyone is doing it these days,' the old woman had insisted, when Aurora did not reply right away. 'If you were allowed to read the books everyone else reads or listen to popular music, you'd know that for yourself.'

So Aurora had plucked up courage. After all, she wanted more than anything to be just like everyone else. She had never seen a needle before — for some strange reason they were forbidden in the palace, though she had overheard the court ladies talk of them — but the old woman had laughed scornfully at her fears.

'It's only a tiny little prick,' she said. 'You'll hardly even feel it at the time. It's the feeling you'll get afterwards, like floating on a cloud of peacock's feathers.'

Aurora thought now that she had said nothing at all about what it would feel like after that. If what the doctor had told her was true, she would make sure any daughter of hers was better prepared than she had been. She had been shut away from every possible danger in order to protect her and it had not protected her at all in the end. It had only made her more vulnerable. It was better to know about everything, she decided. That way you were forewarned.

'Well, well! Just look at the Sleeping Beauty!'

Aurora had been so lost in thought that she had not heard Desie come into the room. She wished he was not always creeping up on her like that in his rubber-soled shoes. Irritated, she kept her eyes closed. Alarmed, Dessie grabbed her arm and examined it closely.

'You've not been main-lining again, have you?' he demanded.

Aurora sat up crossly. 'I have not!' she snapped. 'Will you never accept the fact that I've kicked the habit altogether. I haven't touched drugs of any kind since the day we married.'

'So you keep saying,' Desie said, 'but you can't blame me for worrying.'

'Well, that's lovely, isn't it?' Aurora said sarcastically. 'I mean, it's such a comfort to feel you have so much trust in me.'

'I don't know what you do while I'm out, do I?' Desie said. 'You're here all day by yourself. You could get up to anything.'

Aurora rounded on him. 'And whose fault is that?' she demanded. 'You were the one that refused to let me take a job. What was the point of all those gifts my fairy-godmothers gave me when you won't let me make any use of them? Why did the first fairy give me beauty and the second wit and the third grace and the fourth a voice like a nightingale and . . . .'

Desie signed wearily, and finished the sentence for her. 'And the fifth the ability to dance like Margot Fonteyn and the sixth the gift of playing every musical instrument in the world. I know. I've heard it all till I'm blue in the face.'

44

'So what was the point in all that when you wouldn't even let me play in the panto?'

'My dear girl,' her husband explained patronisingly, 'what would my father's subjects say if the wife of Prince Desiré were to go on the stage?'

'They'd say she had succeeded in spite of her husband's stupid name,' Aurora retorted, making use of the wit given her by her second fairy-godmother which, truth to tell, Desie was not at all sure he considered an asset in a wife.

'Sometimes,' he remarked gratuitously, 'I'm sorry I ever set foot in that wretched forest.'

'And sometimes,' Aurora snapped back, 'I'm sorry that it had to be a selfish chauvinist like you that noticed the tip of the castle turrets above the tops of the trees.'

'So that's all the thanks I get,' Desie shouted, 'for wearing myself out hacking my way through all that undergrowth! If I'd had any sense I'd have left you to sleep for another hundred years.'

'At least I'd have had a little peace,' Aurora shouted back. 'From the time you get home in the evening all you ever do is ask questions: did I do this, have I done that. You want to know what I was doing all afternoon, here on my own? I was thinking, that's what I was doing. It's the only chance I get to think when you're not here!'

'You're not supposed to think,' Desie said calmly. 'If I need any thinking done I can always go to the Court Philosopher. Your job is to look after your husband and bear him children.'

Aurora thought about her interview with the doctor. She had meant to tell Desie about it as soon as he came in, but after the things he had said to her she was not in the humour for it now.

'And suppose I don't want a child?' she asked instead.

Desie looked shocked. 'It's your duty to provide me with an heir,' he said. 'My father's subjects expect it.'

Aurora felt a cold anger fill her from the top of her golden head to the soles of her beautifully-shaped feet. They were all quick enough to say what they expected of *her*, what was *her* duty to Desie. Nobody ever seemed to talk about *his* duty to *her*. She looked at him coldly and wondered how she had ever thought him a desirable husband.

'I'll get the tea,' she said.

As she filled the big copper kettle, she thought again that being a princess was a rotten job. A commoner could have gone home to mother. If she returned to the Court of King Florestan it would mean war between the two kingdoms. It was an absurd custom, nearly everyone thought that now, but it was written into the constitution. One day, maybe, people would wake up and insist on a change. In the meantime, she would just have to go on living with Desie and make the best of a bad job. It was not fair. Why should she suffer for the rest of her life for a decision taken at the age of sixteen, but that was how things were.

She thought ruefully that she would be even more tied to the house once the baby came. She supposed Desie would want a boy, who might one day be king.

She took the bread knife from the drawer and began slicing the royal loaf. She attacked it viciously, as if it were Desie she was slicing into little pieces. She would have to see if she could contact her fairy-godmothers. Maybe they could do something to make sure she had a girl.

'And if I do,' she said out loud, 'they needn't bother giving her beauty and grace and wit and all that nonsense. They'd do a whole lot better to give her strength and dexterity and a good head for figures. And I'll make sure she learns a few skills at the tech. so she won't have to marry a prince for a living!'

Carolyn Swift

Rot So Little Red Riding Hood

I T WAS her mother, not Scarlet, who was in the habit of saying that in November, night arrived in one sudden bound to land on your shoulders and overpower you with blackness. Women in particular were vulnerable then. But Scarlet was not fanciful or concerned that dusk had fallen. As her strides opened out her red cape, she did not pull it closer. Treading crisply on unnoticed twigs, her eyes followed the rooks' ungainly flop into high nests on the tops of oak trees. Each bird harshly squawked out a place for itself before settling down fussily for the night. Scarlet smiled. The laden basket under her arm did not drag her down. It helped her to pace her step as the wide swaying umbrella of the fir trees gradually welcomed her to itself.

A shadow fell. The wolf whistle was so soft and low that she took it for yet another innocent sylvan preparation for rest. She could not join in, even had she been invited. She had to hurry on, so she promptly ignored and forgot about it. But he, the man in the perfectly cut grey suit, would most definitely not be ignored. He stepped out fully and confidently into her path. He leant against the tallest fir, folded his arms and smiled, knowing at least that his front teeth were perfect. Then he wedged his right foot in front of her, in line with the knotted tree root, casually, slowly, as if his mind were elsewhere. The *Irish Times* under his elbow carefully brushed her waist. At that, Scarlet skipped abruptly to the side to pass.

He allowed his eyes to look hurt but not puzzled. They would have been puzzled if this had not happened before. But this wasn't the first time that a girl in a brilliant scarlet cape had led him on. Sometimes it seemed to him that every day of his life women paraded briefly in front of him before letting him down with a bang. At least, to give himself due credit, he had not given up on the entire sex yet.

But Scarlett's peace of mind was now disturbed. The stride had broken into an undignified scurry through the now unwelcoming wood. The wood enclosed her within an embrace of its own. Her breath tightened her body as with a lace. She heard bare branches smack like whips above her head and watched the woody fragments

47

flutter slowly to the ground.

The man in grey took some time to decide the next step. It was that he should become a natural spirit of the wood, back to nature and all that. So he became a spirited animal in its true element swinging down from the branch of a large oak in her path. Scarlet smelt the faint scent of Brut first before she saw the display. But then, standing and smiling, he did not want her to think that he was merely animal. In fact, he went to some pains to dispel any impression of physical over-exuberance. He made quite a show of dusting down his jacket and straightening his collar. He flicked back his tinted hair with carefully manicured nails. Then he busied himself to make an even smaller knot of his tie, a hard little obstacle to everything and nothing. He was ready. Matters were taking their course.

'I hope I didn't startle you.'

Scarlet was still recovering from the shock of seeing a large creature emerge from an oak. She first cast around for her fiercest curse but then settled for irony instead.

'Of course not. What would make you think such a thing?'

He was a little disappointed but soon cheered up.

'Tell you what,' he said, 'you look a bit tired and uptight with all that running in the dark. What's a nice girl like you doing in a place like this anyway? How about a bite to eat and then a good film.'

He paused to give himself time to smile ingratiatingly at her, but she had gone. Now she was just another fleck in the expansive darkness — not a word of thanks, not even a smile. He raged. He wanted to uproot the tree from which he had swung and hurl it at the sky. He wanted not just the wood but the whole universe to know how he had been abused. As a gentleman, he had offered a courteous invitation, but as the card passed from his hand to hers, she had crumbled it to shreds and then simply vanished.

He brought himself slowly up to his full height and threw his head back. But he saw nothing of Scarlet or the wood, nor did he hear the rooks cawing. He ran as he had never run before, as if he were used to fourfootedness. With an unerring instinct, he headed straight for the grandmother's cottage and slunk behind a nearby shrub to wait.

Scarlet was herself again. Striding ahead with the laden basket, she was planning the meal ahead and humming over a new recipe for lentil soup. She had clearly forgotten him already, as if he had been one of life's daily irritants. Black rage bit further into his throat. He decided at once that he would make sure that she never forget him. His body became sheeted steel from which his limbs extended as grappling hooks. He was the last invincible warrior with the ultimate weapon. As he began to grapple, he smiled.

Scarlet said nothing but looked slightly irritated. The task was almost too easy for a karate black belt. But casually and in a leisurely manner, she moved forward to deal him an eye gouge first and then a kick to the groin. Before she could reach for the nerve centre, the solar plexus, it was all over. He had crumbled to pieces and was whimpering for mercy. She flicked him out of her way with her boot and he was grateful for the disdainful, disappearing step.

Scarlet proceeded up her grandmother's path and the man heard the door open to the question 'Had a good day, dear,' and saw Scarlet shrug in answer. When he was able he loped for the lights of the nearest pub, deciding to drown the memory of Scarlet in his pints. It was best for both of them that way really.

Anne Sharpe

No White and the Seven Big Brothers

I T IS now long ago, quite two thousand years, since there was a land where the snow never melted, though the sun shone brightly. In this Land of Snow all women wore white so that it was hard to distinguish one from the other. The seven abominable snowmen had made this law of the land when they had come to power and no one dared challenge them because they were seven Big Brothers.

In the part of the kingdom known as the Glass Valley lived a brave young girl called Noreen who lived in a mountain cottage with her grandmother, Nora. They grew vegetables and ate nuts and berries and made cheese and yoghurt from the milk which came from their seven goats. Nora had grown old and feeble and she could not get about as fast as before. She grew fearful that one day little Noreen would get lost or hurt in the snow and she would not be able to find her. So, although it was against the law of the land, she knit a red cap for Noreen, so that when the child went walking for miles, Nora could spot her easily in the snow. Little Noreen was delighted and promised to wear the cap always to remind her of her grandmother. Day by day, Nora grew more feeble and so she made herself a walking stick. She painted it red and put a silver handle on it and used it till the day she died.

The child Noreen was only seven when this happened so she had to go down the mountain to seek help to bury her grandmother. But when she came into the village the White Guards seized her and brought her to the big White House where the seven Big Brothers ruled.

'Don't you know the law of the land? You must wear white from now on,' the Biggest Brother bellowed. But little Noreen refused. The Big Brothers were furious.

'What? No White? No White?' they all shouted. But Noreen was not afraid. She remembered her grandmother who was dead on the mountain and asked for their help but they would not listen. They gave her one last chance to comply.

'I will wear no white. I will not be faceless or fade into the

background. I will wear no white!' Noreen declared defiantly and from
that day on she was called No White. The seven Big Brothers banished
her to the great Dark Forest for seven years as punishment.

When she arrived in the forest she was cold and lonely and hungry.
But then she recognised some nuts and berries that she used to gather
with her grandmother and she felt a little better. All she could think of
was how to get out and go back up the mountain to her home and her
goats. When she had walked a good many steps she sat down on a log
to rest. She fell asleep and she had a dream in which her grandmother
came alive, wrapped her arms around her and carried her to the top of
the mountain and pointed to the land of the Warm Summer Wind far
far away. This dream made her feel contented and as she woke she
thought she saw her grandmother's smiling face before her. Then she
realised this was a stranger smiling at her and she jumped up in fright.

'Where have you come from, Little Red Cap?' asked the tall woman.

'My name is No White from the Land of Snow and I want to find my
way home to my grandmother's cottage in Glass Valley,' said No
White.

'I am Diana the Huntswoman and I can help you,' said the woman
holding out her hand. 'Come with me and I'll show you the way.'

No White looked keenly at the strange woman who had befriended
her. She was tall and strong. She carried a quiver on her back with lots
of different feathered arrows in it. Her left hand rested on a double

axe in her belt. She wore sheepskins and had a red feather in her hat. No White decided to go with her.

For seven year they travelled through the Dark Forest and Diana taught No White how to hunt and fish and to know which berries and mushrooms were good to eat and which were poisonous. No White learned quickly and soon she knew every birdcall in the forest and every animal by name. She learned how to make paints and dyes from berries and how to build a raft and a shelter and light a fire in the winter.

At the end of seven years it was time for her to leave. Diana took her on a long journey. In a clearing at the heart of the forest they came to a stone gateway. Diana had already told No White what to do. Together they walked in a circle, stamped their feet three times and knocked on the gate chanting:

'I come with Red Feather, I come with Red Cap,

Here I rap, Here I tap,

Here I find the yielding gap.'

The stone gate opened and No White walked through it. There on a stone slab was a red pouch filled with coloured stones with mysterious markings. Diana had told her about these stones. They contained the ancient wisdom of the White Witches and the Legend of the Dark Forest said that one day a snowmaiden would come and unlock their secret. No White chose three stones and put them in her silver pouch. A loud clap of thunder struck and a flash of lightning lit up the stones, so that they glowed like metal or coins. The ground opened and she fell down and down. She closed her eyes in fright and when she opened them she found herself inside a cave. She stood for a moment staring in wonder at the red arched tunnels with the fiery glow and heard a sharp sound. When she turned around Diana had disappeared. Fear gripped her but then she heard Diana's voice whispering.

'Keep to the Left. No matter what you meet or who you greet do not be enticed to the Right Wing of the cave. Fear not the Might of the Right. Travel on but beware of the Ghoulish Fools.'

Hardly had she taken a step on her path when out came Hansel on her right hand:

'I bring greetings from Hansel and Gretel

Behold our House of Sweetness and Light

With everything neat and much to eat

Give me but one portion of your fine metal

And here you may settle.'

No White peered down the path to the Right and saw a wondrous sight, a house built of bread and cakes. The roof was made of chocolate and the windows were clear sugar. No White had not eaten during her long journey through the forest and she was very hungry.

'Come with me. Just have a taste,' said Hansel beckoning her. He broke off a piece of the roof and offered it to her. A voice said:

'Nibble, nibble, gnaw, gnaw

Who is nibbling at my door?'

'Shish!' said Hansel to No White. 'The wind, the wind,' he answered.

'It is not the wind,' said No White. 'It's you.'

'Who?' said a woman's voice, on her left. 'Ah, I thought so. Don't eat that.'

'I wasn't going to,' said No White a little unsettled by all these quick changes on her life's path. 'And who are you?'

'I'm Gretel of course. You must be Alice.'

'No I'm not. I'm No White from the Land of Snow!'

'And to the Land of Snow you go . . .' said Gretel and she opened her mouth wide and gave a big whistle and a whoosh, which sent all three of them rolling back down the tunnel onto the Left hand path.

Hansel giggled and snickered while Gretel explained that he was always trying to sell the house over her head but in fact it was *her* house. It was made from all the food she could not eat when she used to go on diets. She had the brilliant idea of stacking the food in the shape of a house and putting a glaze on it.

No White thanked Gretel for helping her and away she went. But no sooner had she drawn another breath when out popped a handsome prince from a rat hole on the right. He squeaked:

'I am Rumpelstilskin, what do you think?

I offer you my heart and my kitchen sink

My video, my stereo, my carpets and my car

My bells do chime, my words do rhyme,

Give me but one portion of your fine metal

And here you may settle.'

No White had never seen such a psychedelic sight. She looked in awe and paused for thought and got another fright when out came the prince's mother who cried 'Oh Brother!'

'Is he trying to catch you? Did he show you his statue?

But he forgot his mother, a penny farthing Spinner

And he'll forget you too once he's found another Winner

Do not marry, do not tarry,

Do not stay another day
But pray thee, go your own sweet way.'
No White turned to shake hands with the mother but did not see her sewing needle and she pricked her finger. Her head was spinning as she ran back down the tunnel. She breathed a sigh of relief when she found her way out to her own path again.

This part of the cave was dimly lit and growing darker. No White was tired and hungry. She was feeling miserable and weepy and when she came to a fork in the tunnel she turned to the left and found herself faced with seven paths. Three paths to the right, three paths to the left and one in the middle. But which left turn should she take?

The paths looked like the spokes of a wheel. The wheel began to spin and with each revolution she became more confused. She thought 'Stop! I want to get off!' No sooner had she thought it than it came to pass. All her frantic activity stopped. Where was she? This was an unfamiliar country. The cave seemed to be lit up on all sides with all the colours of the rainbow. She looked to the right and a crock of gold appeared. She looked to the left and an Ancient Book of Wisdom appeared. She looked down at her finger. The pain had gone. The blood had stopped and she thought she saw a thimble on the tip but looking closer she realised it was a little man, in a tin hat, or was it a drum? He seemed to be shouting but she could not hear. She raised her finger to her ear and he said:

'I'm Tom Thumb I play my drum
I'm fumblesome and frolicsome
My house is free and here's the key
Give me but one portion of your fine metal
And here you may settle.'

No White was enthralled. She put her ear to the ground and listened to Tom's jokes. He made her laugh. She saw him poking at something in his awkward amusing fashion. He gave her a microscope to look through the keyhole of his house. She saw jugglers, acrobats and clowns, people dressed up in all sorts of guises, some kings and queens and fairies with glittering diamonds. Everyone was happy, cheerful and gay. They seemed to be performing just for her. She laughed till she cried. The tears wet her hand and the stones became slippery in her palm. The curtain came down on the cabaret and then she heard the compere paying tribute to the Ghoulish Fools and everyone laughed. No White felt a chill as she remembered Diana's warning. She put the stones back in her pouch and rubbed them together. Instantly a golden cloud enveloped her and she flew high above the caves, above the forest, above the snow and came to land at a golden bridge. Diana Red Feather was waiting on the other side on a white horse. She hailed No White:

'No White, No White pray do not tarry
We must parry Tom, Dick and Harry.'

No White climbed quickly into the saddle in front of her. They rode for seven days and seven nights and when they reached the Land of Snow, No White's red cap had become a long red riding cape with a hood. Diana gave No White her double axe and explained:

'Now that you, No White, have fulfilled your destiny and freed the Summer Wind it blows across the land and all the snow is melting. The Big Brothers are losing their grip. But to try to hold on to their power they have captured the Seven Spinsters who refused to wear white on their wedding day and they have encased them in ice coffins high in the mountains. At present they are sleeping. You and I must free them before they die.'

Diana pressed her heels sharply against the horse's flanks and the great white mare galloped off faster than the wind until they arrived at Three Rock mountain. No White and Diana climbed and climbed

55

but when they reached the peak the Big Brothers had got there before them. They were crestfallen until suddenly, near a tree, No White saw a familiar piece of wood. It was Nora's red stick with the silver handle. She knew she was near her old home. They crept round the mountain and there, with the snow still on the roof and the goats still grazing outside, stood her grandmother's house. Something inside her told her to put the magic stones in the hearth and light a fire. When she did, the magic smoke enveloped the seven Big Brothers who smothered and died on the spot.

Diana fixed her eyes on the ice coffins as she stretched her bow to its full breadth. Each of the seven arrows struck home. No White wielded her double axe to cut through the glass-like casings, splitting the ice cleanly each time. She stood in wide-eyed wonder as the Seven Spinsters came back to life. Diana hugged her and No White placed her labrys back in her belt with pride.

The Spinsters carried the remains of No White's grandmother's body to the top of the mountain. They placed her bones between three rocks and pushed one forward with all their might. Then they used sharp stones to make a pattern of seven spirals on the rock facing south. Diana and No White joined hands with them to form a circle. The nine women chanted Nora's name, their voices carrying far on the wind. Then, magically, the three rocks moved closer together and the burial mound was complete.

Diana explained to No White that in olden times when someone died, especially a Wise Old Woman like her grandmother, people were sad. But they also knew that her time had come to join the spirit world of Tir na nOg, where she would become young again, so they rejoiced and held a merry wake. Hearing this, No White decided to invite Diana and the Spinsters to celebrate Nora's passing in the old way. The nine stayed in No White's house feasting and ceili dancing for nine days and nine nights.

And on the Summer Solstice, the Summer Wind blew across the land for the first time in two thousand years and all was well.

Joni Crone

Cinderella Re-examined

ONCE upon a time there were three sisters whose appearance is immaterial but the eldest girl Thunder had a ferocious temper, and a great greed for money. She was constantly scanning the papers and magazines to find out where she might be likely to meet wealthy men. 'Don't love for money' she warned the others. 'But love where money is.'

The second sister was called Lightning, and she wasn't as obsessed with wealth as Thunder was, but she had plenty to keep her busy. Lightning had this very firm belief that you never got a husband, wealthy or impoverished unless you played a game by the rules, and the rules were to promise everything and deliver nothing. Lightning had been called some very unattractive names in her time, but she just laughed because she said those kind of men weren't husband material anyway.

Thunder and Lightning had a younger sister who was called Cinderella, she didn't have any very firm philosophy like they did, so they thought she was a bit dull. Cinderella ran the house for the family and without much complaint so Thunder and Lightning thought she was a bit wet as well. But Cinderella shrugged and said what the hell, Father had given Thunder the money to open a boutique and he had given Lightning the money to set up a beauty shop, and he wouldn't hear of giving Cinderella the money to buy the franchise for a Fast Food chain which is what she wanted, so she might as well make the best of it until she had enough money of her own one day. She seemed to enjoy going to the market and buying food in bulk and she was always cheerful. She was doing two correspondence courses as well as a degree from the Open University, and she never crossed the paths of Thunder or Lightning, and Father was pleased to have nice meals put in front of him, so everyone in the household seemed reasonably content.

From time to time, like most families they had disappointments. Cinderella would ask her father to stake her even a small fish and chip shop, but to no avail. Thunder might go on the prowl certain she had found wealthy men only to discover that they were penniless fortune hunters. Very often Lightning's date of the evening drove away in a terrible rage. But nothing more serious than that disturbed their peaceful ways.

Then one day all hell broke loose. It was the day when thev announced that the king was going to give a huge ball at the palace and his handsome playboy son who had broken many hearts but without managing to make any commitments whatsoever was going to be there and the gossip columns all said that the prince was going to make a determined effort to find a wife at last, having tried everything else that the world could offer, there were few areas of mystery left to him and he was going to begin the long and responsible process of settling down. Thunder was in a frenzy of excitement. When she had hoped to marry wealth she had never dared to set her sights as high as the prince, but after all why not? She was after all a highly fashionable woman. She settled like a storm cloud in her boutique and organised it so that all her customers who might be rivals got hideous clothes while her own outfit was a dazzler. Lightning felt that she now had the whole thing sewn up. What these other foolish hussies had done wrong was to give their all to the prince when he looked like needing it. Lightning was going to tempt the prince out of his poor simple basic mind. She hired a plastic surgeon for her beauty salon in order to make her own bosom more curvaceous than ever. At the same time the plastic surgeon was to disimprove any clients that might be rivals. Not disfigure them but dull them up a bit. Cinderella wasn't at all interested in the ball, she thought it was mildly interesting in a sociological way, but she hadn't much time to concentrate on it on account of doing several papers which had all come up at once in her correspondence courses, and entering a competition in a magazine. There was some ridiculous Charm Course or something as first prize but there were six runner-up prizes of nice sums of money and since Father still wouldn't agree to listen to her financial proposals, she knew she would have to find the money herself. It seemed a silly sort of competition but still, it was only the cost of a stamp. So Cinderella did it.

Six weeks before the great ball at the palace Cinderella was visited by a most extraordinary looking woman, in an insane looking tiara. There was also a photographer who started to take pictures of Cinderella opening the door and the idiotic woman in the net dress and the silly thing on her head started to whimper and cry out that Cinderella had won the Amazing Charm Course worth hundreds and hundreds of pounds. Cinderella discussed it long and earnestly but

she met with diamond hard opposition from the magazine columnist who called herself Fairy Godmother. F.G. was in fact deeply affronted that Cinderella wanted to sell her Charm Course to the highest bidder, she wouldn't even countenance offering Cinderella a cash prize. It was the Charm Course or nothing. Cinderella decided it must be nothing, she had no time to learn to walk gracefully, how to swing her legs out of a car, how to eat cake without making crumbs. She was quite happy to put some make-up on her face but she felt her allotted lifespan was much too short to waste any of it learning about drawing hollows in her cheeks and how to apply loose powder and then dust most of it off. As politely as she could she thanked F.G., the Fairy Godmother, and said she had to go back to her studies.

'You also get an Art Appreciation Course, a Music Course and a Five easy steps to Bluffing your way in Literature Course' said the awful F.G., 'and lots of books and records and pictures as well.'

Cinderella got out her pocket calculator. She could sell the books, records and pictures. There would be a small profit in it. She would do it.

The household continued reasonably happily, Thunder rolling unmercifully around her boutique, Lightning flashing round her beauty salon and Cinderella yawning her way through Care of the Cuticles and what to pack for a weekend houseparty.

'Do pay attention Cinderella,' said the head of the Charm Course. 'You're going to need all this when you go to the ball.'

'Oh no I haven't any intention of going to the ball,' Cinderella said and she had to sit down suddenly and inelegantly from shock when she realised that part of the prize she had won involved her going to the ball decked in borrowed jewellery and furs and travelling in a big sleek ˙car which was hers for the night only. She would be photographed in all her finery and girls everywhere would envy her the wonderful opportunities she had won.

'But it's going to be a very boring evening, and I'll be worried about all this gear that doesn't belong to me,' Cinderella began. Nonsense, they wouldn't listen to her. Everyone in the country was positively aching for such a chance. Cinderella felt depressed when it was put to her that way but agreed that she had better shut up and go along with it, it would all be over soon and she could sell these immense coffrets of cosmetics and a lot of other over priced goods that didn't interest her.

Thunder and Lightning were so busy in their own preparations for the Ball that it never occurred to them to ask Cinderella if she was going or not, and they were most aggrieved when the big car turned up to collect her. Cinderella offered them a lift, she said reasonably that there was room for half the street in it but Lightning and Thunder said of course they weren't going to arrive, three girls together, it would be pathetic. They looked suspiciously at Cinderella's appearance which seemed to have improved very deceitfully. Her dress and extraordinary elegant glass shoes took them by surprise.

'It's all part of the prize, remember the Fairy Godmother prize,' Cinderella tried to explain but Thunder's brow darkened and Lightning's eyes flashed and they went back to their own rooms for final titivation in very bad tempers indeed.

The man from the car firm said the car had to be back by twelve midnight, and the furrier said that he had to have his mink back then too otherwise it wouldn't be properly insured, the jeweller said he had to put the diamond necklace into a night safe at midnight, and Cinderella said that was all fine, the sooner the better as far as she was concerned.

The palace was big and draughty and even though they had gone to great trouble setting out a banquet, a lot of the food was cold by the time it had gone the long journey through the stone corridors. There was a great amount of waste Cinderella noticed, not to mention thieving. She could see that one of the fellows in a powdered wig who was meant to be in charge had a nice little number going for himself with boxes and bags which were being taken out as if they were rubbish but were in fact full of first rate food waiting to be loaded onto a waiting lorry.

The king was old and had a sad smile. He hoped that everyone was having a good time and that the prince might lay off the booze a bit and try to focus on some of the young women, preferably a young woman with a great deal of money, since the palace was near financial ruin. The reason behind this very extravagant ball was the hope of ensnaring the daughter of a self-made millionaire who would be so thrilled about the Royal connection that every bill would be paid unquestioningly. Wouldn't that be great? The king sighed heavily.

Cinderella was near him as he sighed and she felt sorry for him.

'It must have been a desperate job organising this lot,' she said sympathetically.

'It was,' said the king, 'and it cost a fortune.'

'It could have been a bit better organised,' said Cinderella.

'Well we spent months organising it,' said the king sadly, 'and do you know I think they're running low on wine, and there must have been thousands of pounds worth of strawberries and they didn't stretch at all.'

'Oh, they stretched all right,' Cinderella said. 'If you asked someone from security to look out in the back yard, you'd see them stretching into refrigerated lorries.'

That was the start of it. The king was delighted with Cinderella. She took him on a tour of his own palace and pointed out how savings

could be made.

She explained that the old fashioned kitchen was losing him more money than he could imagine, she indicated where the freezers should be, how stores should be kept. She took out her pocket calculator from her small silver handbag and did some sums, as she thought it would be quite possible for the palace to go into the business of serving food to visitors.

The king became very excited, he took off his crown and Cinderella took off the glass slippers that were crucifying her and together they planned a turn around in the palace finances. So engrossed did they become that it was midnight and the furriers and jewellers and car people were hysterical crying to repossess their property. Casually Cinderella peeled off the diamonds, gave them the car keys and her cloakroom ticket for the mink. She and the king talked on but in order not to be anti-social, they went back to the ballroom. The prince spotted Cinderella towards the end of the ball and asked her to dance.

'Oh please, please do,' said the king, hoping that by some wild chance his dim son might marry this financial wizard and keep her in the family.

The prince danced well if drunkenly. Cinderella said it was like walking on knives trying to dance in those shoes so she took them off again and left them under a table out of the way. Without actually seeing her sisters she could feel the disapproval of Thunder and Lightning, but the prince was so boring that Cinderella excused herself and left the floor, she could only find one of her shoes but decided it was not worth hunting for the other. They were dangerous anyway and she was going to have a word with the manufacturers about them. She said goodbye to the king and hitched a lift home.

The gossip columns were full of the prince's agony. He had met the one true love of his life and all he had to remember her by and even to identify her by was a glass slipper. The papers made a meal out of it.

Cinderella rang him up and asked him to stop being so crass and to examine his own assumptions that anyone would make an effort to find a glass slipper and try to win him just because he was a prince. She said that if he would forgive plain speaking he should watch the gargle as well, and while she was on the phone could he get his father for there were a few more things she had intended to say to him.

The prince was very peeved and even more so when he noticed Cinderella was in a short time a regular visitor to the palace, and then an employee and was soon in charge of the entire catering side of things. The prince admitted that the coffee was fresh, good and hot, which it had never been before. The food was excellent, and the palace was open to visitors three afternoons a week, which brought in a great deal of revenue. Cinderella and the king were hatching up more and more ideas. There were plans for a conference centre. The king was going to give a lot of the land to the Corpo to make it into a public park, and this meant the king did not have to pay the gardeners, the Corpo did, and everyone seemed pleased.

The prince kept the glass slipper in his briefcase along with his vodka and white lemonade. Occasionally he would take it out and stroke the glass and wish he was the kind of man Cinderella would marry.

He was sitting playing with the shoe one day when Cinderella came in.

'I really think you should see someone about this foot fetish you have,' she said to him kindly. 'I'm sure it's something they could cure.'

'Please, please will you marry me,' burst out the prince.

'No thank you,' said Cinderella courteously. 'I prefer to be free you see. But I'd like you to think of me as a friend or an advisor.'

'Friend! What kind of friend are you to me? Putting me off the drink, trying to drag me to a shrink saying I've got a thing about feet. That's not friendship.'

Cinderella gently took the shoe away from the prince, she held it up to the light.

'Listen here, Prince, why don't you help us, the group that are trying to get shoes like this banned, crippling young girls' feet, and lethal too. Suppose somebody kicked you in a glass slipper. It could cut the feet off you, just like that.'

The prince looked up with dulled eyes. 'I suppose it's a bit like the Chinese foot binding,' he said.

'Now,' cried Cinderella triumphantly. 'That's better. Come to the protest meeting on Tuesday. Your name on the paper will be a help and it will give you something to do, take you out of the house a bit, bring out out of yourself.'

The prince looked happier than he had for weeks. He was not a bad boy but Cinderella thought she had done the right thing in refusing to marry him. A woman had enough to do these days without taking on a husband who had to be given things to do to keep him occupied. Besides, her post as Chief Executive of Palace Enterprises was going to keep her busy and very happy ever after.

Maeve Binchy

64